Bailey
the Babysitter
Fairy

Special thanks to
Mandy Archer

No part of this publication may be reproduced, stored in a retrieval system, or transmitted in any form or by any means, electronic, mechanical, photocopying, recording, or otherwise, without written permission of the publisher. For information regarding permission, write to Rainbow Magic Limited, c/o HIT Entertainment, 830 South Greenville Avenue, Allen, TX 75002-3320.

ISBN 978-0-545-60539-7

Previously published as *Jennifer the Babysitter Fairy* by Orchard U.K. in 2013.

All rights reserved. Published by Scholastic Inc., 557 Broadway, New York, NY 10012, by arrangement with Rainbow Magic Limited.

12 11 10 9 8 7 6 5 4 3 2   17 18 19/0

Printed in the U.S.A.   40

First printing, May 2014

Bailey
the Babysitter Fairy

by Daisy Meadows

SCHOLASTIC INC.

The Fairyland Palace

Fairyland Nursery

EcoWorld

Eco-Lodges

Kirsty and Rachel's Lodge

Treetop Café

Jack Frost's
Ice Castle

Eco-Domes

← Splash
Park

Sunnydays
Kids' Club

← Supermarket

Jack Frost's Spell

Goblins botch and goblins fumble,
Goblins shout and goblins grumble,
Got to fix this naughty rabble,
Stuck out tongues and noisy babble.

All babysitters should beware,
I'll snatch the objects in your care,
Precious things from precious tots,
As they lie curled up in their cots.

**Find the hidden letters in the star shapes
throughout this book. Unscramble
all 8 letters to spell a special word!**

Toy Box
Trouble

Contents

Vacation Begins!

"Rachel, look!" Kirsty Tate gasped, peeking out of the lodge window. "We can see the butterfly house from our bedroom!"

Rachel Walker dropped her suitcase and ran around to the other side of the bed. As soon as she pulled back the polka-dot print curtain, her face lit up with a smile.

"I can see it!" she replied. There, almost hidden among the trees, was a cluster of cabins and greenhouses in all different shapes and sizes. The butterfly house was the one in the middle, next to the main eco-center. Inside, tropical plants and flowers curled up toward the sunshine, filling the dome with rainbow colors.

It was the perfect beginning to the girls' spring break. Kirsty and Rachel had only just arrived, but they loved it here already! Their families had organized this weekend away at the EcoWorld activity center—an amazing park set in the heart of a leafy forest. Mr. and Mrs. Tate's friends, the Robinsons, had been invited, too.

Everything at EcoWorld had been carefully designed to protect the animals and plants that lived in the countryside around it. The Tates, Walkers, and Robinsons were spending the weekend in a pretty eco-lodge built out of reclaimed wood. Everything in the park was recycled, even the water in the swimming pools!

Kirsty picked up her EcoWorld

brochure and started flicking through the pages. "Should we go exploring?" she asked. "It says there's a climbing wall and a rain forest area and . . . wow! Rachel, the dome over the man-made lake has a roof that opens up when it's sunny!"

Rachel couldn't help but giggle—she'd grabbed her fleece already! She and Kirsty had only three precious days together and she wanted to make the most of every minute.

"I wonder what we'll find today?" she mused.

Kirsty's eyes twinkled. She and Rachel were used to discovering all kinds of amazing, magical things. The lucky girls shared a secret—they were friends with the fairies! The pair had been on some incredible adventures. Jack Frost and his goblins were always stomping into Fairyland and trying to stir up trouble. If a fairy needed their help, they only had to wave their magic wand and Rachel and Kirsty would be there.

The girls slipped on their fleeces and scampered out into the yard. The lodge had large glass doors that opened onto a daisy-speckled lawn.

"Kirsty! Kirsty!" chimed a little voice. "Play! Play!" piped up another.

Kirsty and Rachel beamed at each other. The friends moved aside the branches of a pretty weeping willow and spotted Tom and Lily, Mr. and Mrs. Robinson's two-year-old twins. The toddlers were playing in a sandbox made out of recycled railroad ties.

"Hello, you two!" exclaimed Kirsty. "This is my best friend, Rachel."

"Ra-ra," cooed Lily.

Rachel bent down to meet the excited twins. Lily played peekaboo behind her hands, but Tom gave her a wide smile.

Tom glanced at Lily, then shyly presented their new friend with a shiny orange shovel.

"We can't play right now, Tom," Kirsty said kindly, "but we'll come back and build sand castles later."

Rachel nodded. "We just want to see

what there is to do in EcoWorld."

The adorable little boy clapped his hands. He'd spotted Mrs. Tate wandering up to the sandbox with his bottle. Kirsty's mom pulled a crumpled list and some money out of her jeans pocket.

"Can you pick me up a few things from the supermarket?" she asked. "Just follow the signs. The park is totally enclosed, so you can't get lost. Use the change to treat yourselves to a shake at the café afterward if you want."

"Great!" Kirsty grinned.

She linked arms with Rachel, steering her toward a path at the bottom of the yard.

"Isn't this amazing?" remarked Rachel, as the friends stepped onto a maze of boardwalks. Every so often, the walkway would turn a corner, revealing a building nestled in the trees.

The friends rushed to the supermarket and picked out Mrs. Tate's groceries. Soon they were sitting in the Treetop Café, each clutching a tasty milk shake.

"I'll get some straws," offered Kirsty, spotting a container in the corner.

She lifted the lid and picked out two straws with glittering stripes. She took them back to the table.

Rachel blinked, then peered around the café. Was she imagining it, or did her straw seem to be sparkling more brightly than everyone else's?

A Fairy Friend in Need

The sparkly straw was shimmering brilliantly now. Kirsty had never seen a straw twinkle before—it had to be fairy magic! Rachel propped the straw against her milk shake so that no one else in the café could see it.

"Thank you!" trilled a sweet singsong voice. "I've been waiting for you to arrive."

A tiny fairy stepped out from behind the milk shake glass. She was wearing denim shorts, cropped leggings, and a red scarf dotted with yellow polka dots. Her blonde hair swished as she moved, drawing attention to her spray of freckles.

"My name is Bailey the Babysitter Fairy," she said, waving a tiny hand. "I work in the Fairyland Nursery."

"We're so pleased to meet you!" gasped Kirsty. "I'm Kirsty, by the way, and this is Rachel."

Bailey nodded her head, but her smile seemed sad.

"I know all about you both," she replied, "and everything that you've done for the fairies. That's why I came here today."

"Is something wrong?" Rachel asked quietly.

Bailey's eyes filled with tears. Something was definitely wrong.

"It's my job to look after the fairy babies," she explained, before adding, "Not on my own, of course. All of the fairies take turns to help in the Fairyland Nursery. The Sports Fairies are always coming by to play games and the Rainbow Fairies love sharing their colorful spells."

"That sounds wonderful," said Kirsty.

"It is," replied Bailey. "Or at least it was . . . until Jack Frost stole my three magic objects!"

"The rain forest zone is next door,"  suggested Rachel. "Let's find a quiet place where we can talk in private."

Kirsty agreed. She helped Bailey climb into the shopping bag so they could smuggle her outside.

The girls slipped out of the café and tiptoed into the damp, warm air of the rain forest dome. The huge glass pod was alive with jungle plants—from towering trees to stunning tropical flowers. Every few moments a

light shower of rain sprinkled down from special hoses in the ceiling.

"Over here," said Rachel, pointing toward a little glade hidden by giant palms.

When they were sure that the coast was clear, Bailey flew out of the shopping bag. She fluttered like a butterfly in a circle around the girls, her golden wings lighting up the shadows.

"Fairyland is in terrible trouble," she said urgently. She settled next to a puddle of rainwater, then touched it with her wand. The puddle began to swirl and cloud over.

Kirsty nudged Rachel—Bailey was creating a magic Seeing Pool! The water cleared, revealing a cheerful playroom decorated with colorful pictures and twinkly lights. Along one end were ten tiny cribs, each covered with a chiffon canopy trimmed with the finest fairy embroidery.

"This is the
Fairyland
Nursery,"
said Bailey,
peering
sadly into
the water.
"Usually
it's full of happy
fairy babies."
Rachel's heart leaped.

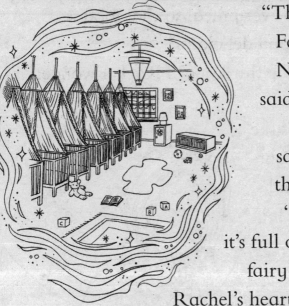

In all of their adventures together, the
girls had *never* met any fairy babies!

"What are those?" asked Kirsty,
pointing to three quilted cushions.

"That's where I keep my precious
objects!" replied Bailey. "The magic toy
box makes sure that everyone enjoys
their playtimes. The magic lunch bag

enchants every meal so that food is healthy and delicious."

"And the third one?" Rachel wondered out loud.

"That's the magic night-light," said Bailey. "It helps all babies have restful naps and sweet  dreams at bedtime. The poor kids will be worn out without it!"

The troubled fairy began to shed silvery tears. As they dropped into the water, each one made the tiniest tinkling sound.

"Please don't cry," said Kirsty.

"Between the three of us, we'll get your magic objects back. Won't we, Rachel?"

Rachel nodded her head as hard as she could. "Of course we will!" she agreed. "When did they disappear?" "This afternoon," Bailey answered, "in the middle of story time."

Suddenly, the rain forest water began to shine like a mirror. The girls saw the Fairyland Nursery again, but now it was full of adorable fairy babies. The little ones were sitting in a circle,

gurgling happily. Bailey was reading a
fairy story, conjuring up floating pictures
with her wand.

"Look!" Kirsty gasped, pointing to the
back of the playroom.

Three goblins were climbing in
through the window, each disguised as a
giant baby! The silly threesome
pretended to crawl across a rug,
mumbling baby noises under their
breath.

"Goo-goo, ga-ga!" babbled one, hitching up a badly fastened diaper.

"Babies are yucky," grumbled his friend. "This is the grossest thing Jack Frost has ever made us do!"

"Be quiet!" snapped the third. "Just grab the gear and let's go!"

Kids' Club Chaos

Kirsty looked up from the pool and frowned. "So the goblins stole the three magic objects and took them back to Jack Frost's Ice Castle?" she asked sadly.

Bailey's wings drooped a little lower. "No," she said. "They decided to cause some trouble first! The goblins thought it would be very funny to hide the objects instead. My precious things could be anywhere by now."

Rachel gulped. Without the magic toy box, lunch bag, and night-light, children in both the fairy and human worlds wouldn't be very happy at all.

"Let's start looking right away," she declared. "Babies need sleep, good food, and playtime. We can't let Jack Frost and his goblins spoil those things!"

"I knew you'd be able to help!" Bailey beamed. "I'll go back to Fairyland and search for clues there. I need to check on the nursery, too. The Party Fairies are looking after the babies this afternoon.

They love it when
Melodie the
Music Fairy
sings to
them!"

Bailey
disappeared
in a shimmer
of scarlet fairy
dust.

Kirsty and
Rachel rushed
back to their lodge,
running down the forest
paths as fast as their legs could carry
them. Both were wondering the same
thing—why would Jack Frost steal a
babysitter fairy's enchanted objects? It
didn't make any sense.

"Lily! Tom! What's gotten into you today?"

As they slipped through the front gate, Kirsty and Rachel could only just make out Mrs. Robinson's voice — her words were being drowned out by terrible screeching! The twins were sitting in the middle of the lawn, thumping their little fists.

"That's not like them," whispered Kirsty. "And what happened to all the toys?"

Rachel's mouth fell open. The yard was an absolute mess! The rakes and shovels in the sandbox had been snapped in half, the trampoline had a hole in it, and the twins' soccer ball had deflated. Tom and Lily's parents were crouching down next to the toddlers, desperately

trying to calm them down.

"I don't know how it happened." Mr.
Robinson shrugged. "Every toy they
touched just fell apart!"

The girls shared a secret glance. They
both had a very good idea what was
going on! Until Bailey's magic toy box
was back where it belonged, no one
would be able to enjoy playtime.

"Why don't we take the twins to the
kids' club for a couple of hours?" Rachel
suggested, handing over the groceries.

"Then you'll have a chance to get things cleaned up."

Mrs. Robinson nodded her head gratefully.

"Thank you, girls," agreed Mr. Robinson. "I think that will do us *all* good."

Rachel took Lily's hand and led her out toward the trail at the bottom of the yard. Kirsty followed behind with Tom. With two grouchy toddlers in tow, it took longer to get to the center of the park than last time.

"Here we are!" announced Kirsty, finally spotting the SUNNYDAYS KIDS' CLUB sign.

The girls led the twins into a colorful reception area. Once Tom and Lily had been signed in, a playworker named

Diane came out to greet them.

"The toddlers are playing outside," she said wearily, showing her guests out to a walled garden decorated with cheery murals of ladybugs and bumblebees.

The garden was filled with children, but no one seemed to be having fun. The arts and crafts area on the patio was covered with toppled easels and snapped paintbrushes. On the lawn, a group of children was squabbling over a container of bubbles.

"Yuck!" cried Lily as a bubble popped on her sweater, covering her outfit in sticky goo.

"Oh, dear." Diane sighed. "The children are a little rowdy today."

Kirsty noticed a little boy snatching his friend's trike. In another corner of the garden, two girls fought over a teddy bear.

"We could give you a hand," she offered. "It must be hard looking after all these children on your own."

"I would love some help," replied Diane, "but I'm not on my own. I have a new nursery assistant on toddler duty, but he doesn't seem to be very focused."

Diane pointed to the waterplay area. There, in the middle of the mayhem, a figure stood in one of the troughs. Instead of calming down the toddlers, he was kicking water all over the ground.

Kirsty narrowed her eyes. She couldn't help but notice the stranger's long, pointy nose.

"Rachel!" she whispered. "We've found our first goblin!"

The Goblin Babysitter

As soon as Diane had led the twins off to find aprons, Rachel and Kirsty crept up for a closer look.

"That's a goblin, all right!" whispered Rachel, ducking down behind a slide.

The goblin wore a baseball cap pulled down low and an apron tied around his middle, but his big green feet were a dead giveaway! Instead of having fun in the water, the goblin was muttering furiously under his breath.

"Pesky children!" he hissed. "I turn my back for one minute and they run off with the toy box. Now my toes are all soggy!"

Kirsty winked at her best friend— Bailey's magic object had to be nearby!

"Where could it be?" Kirsty wondered.

"We have to get to the toy box before the goblin does."

As the girls were thinking, a soft breeze blew through their hair and tickled their cheeks. Sunbeams began to dance in the air, glinting brighter and brighter until— *pop!*—Bailey the Babysitter Fairy appeared!

"Is there any news?" she asked anxiously, perching on the edge of the playhouse.

Kirsty and Rachel

told the little fairy all about the grumpy
goblin.

"Good work!" she chirped, her face
flushing with relief. "I just knew that the
magic toy box wasn't too
far away."

Bailey couldn't resist
taking to the skies for
an impromptu loop-
the-loop, her golden
wings glinting in the
afternoon sun.

"We still need to find it,"
Rachel reminded her in a low voice.
She pointed over to the water trough.
The sight of the noisy goblin was enough
to get poor Bailey in a flutter again.

"Let's start looking," she cried. "The
magic toy box has a yellow lid and pink

panels on the sides."

"We'll have a better chance if we split up," suggested Kirsty. "Should I start out here?"

The friends agreed. Bailey flew up to the very top of the playhouse so she could see across the garden, while Rachel tiptoed inside.

The nursery was certainly quieter than the garden, but the children were just as unsettled. In the cozy corner, a flustered assistant was trying to read a fairy tale to a group of unruly listeners.

"Please *try* and pay attention," she begged. "Otherwise you won't find out what happened to Cinderella when the clock struck twelve."

"Don't care!" snapped a little boy, sticking out his tongue.

The assistant turned the page and did her best to continue.

"'And then the wicked witch appeared . . .'" she read, before blurting out, "Wicked witch? There is no wicked witch in *Cinderella*!"

As the assistant grappled with the
confused pages, Rachel began to search
through the toys at the back of the room.
Kirsty soon joined her.

"Let's start over here," Rachel
whispered, pulling out a drawer marked
FARM ANIMALS. "Oh!"

Instead of farm animals, the drawer
was crammed with mixed-up pieces of
jigsaw puzzles. The next one
down was labeled
DINOSAURS, but
there were only
broken toy cars
inside, gummed
together with
play clay.

"Where can
it be?" Rachel

sighed. "We have to find it!"

On the cushions, the toddlers had started to wail. One frustrated little girl even threw her fleecy blanket across the carpet! Rachel ran over to pick it up, stooping down next to a wooden play kitchen.

"Here you go." She smiled, handing the blanket back.

The little girl didn't look up. She was too busy peering at something sparkly inside the kitchen's oven.

"Oh, my!" Rachel gasped, rushing to

get her friends. "I think we've found the magic toy box!"

As soon as Bailey appeared, the girls dashed over to the kitchen.

"Open the door," urged Bailey. "Please hurry."

Rachel reached out for the oven, but a knobbly, green hand bumped her out of the way.

"Only Sunnydays workers allowed in the play area," grunted the goblin. "Hands off!"

Toddlers to the Rescue!

The goblin threw his head back and laughed.

"Ha-ha!" he roared. "You girls can't outsmart me! I'm the best worker in this whole kids' club!"

Kirsty glanced around the playroom. Luckily, the poor assistant was busy trying to tape the pages of her storybook back in the right order.

"Bailey," she whispered quietly, "would you like to hide behind me?"

"Yes, please!" gasped the nervous little fairy, darting into the strands of Kirsty's ponytail.

Rachel stepped forward to plead with the goblin, but he didn't seem to care about the trouble he'd caused.

"Serves the kids right for being so horrible!" he crowed, blowing a big raspberry. "Human children give me the creeps. And babies! Babies are the worst!"

The goblin was so pleased with himself

he did a dance on the spot, kicking his feet in crazy directions.

"Look! Look!"

The toddlers in the cozy corner had stopped crying. One by one they sat-up and stared at the goblin's dance. The children began to clap their hands and point at the funny stranger.

"You are right," said Rachel, with a twinkle in her eye. "You really *are* the best playworker. Look at all the children!"

"What?" asked the goblin, spinning on his heel.

The toddlers had formed a circle around the goblin, their chubby cheeks pink from laughing. A little girl tugged on his apron and tried to hold his hand. Another boy tried to copy the goblin's dance by stamping his feet and wiggling his bottom.

"Help!" cried the goblin, shuddering at the sight of so many thrilled faces. "I'm under attack!"

The goblin shot into the air, but the children just laughed even harder. From her secret hiding spot, Bailey couldn't help giggling, too.

"He looks so terrified of those little kids," she trilled. "How silly!"

The goblin couldn't bear it a moment longer. Rachel and Kirsty watched as he stumbled outside, waving his arms in terror. The children thought it was the best game ever. They toddled after him as fast as they could.

"Well, that's something I've never seen before," remarked Kirsty. "He's the goblin Pied Piper!"

The last thing the friends saw of the new assistant was a shaky figure clambering over the garden wall.

"I think Diane's new recruit has just resigned," said Rachel, opening the play kitchen's oven door. Inside was a glittering toy box with a brilliant yellow lid and bright pink sides.

"That's it!" cried Bailey. "That's my magic toy box!"

The delighted fairy fluttered out into the open in a flurry of twinkling stars. She touched the edge of the toy box with her  wand and it flew into her arms. Bailey hugged the precious object to her, then blew each of the girls a heartfelt thank-you kiss.

"Now the children can play nicely again," said Rachel.

Kirsty smiled happily. "You'd better whisk the toy box to Fairyland, back where it belongs!"

Bailey agreed, but she had an important job to do first. She thought for a moment, then pointed her wand up to the ceiling.

"Pitter-patter, tiny feet,
Everything be nice and neat!"

There was a flash of gold light so dazzling, Kirsty and Rachel had to close their eyes. When they opened them again, the nursery had been transformed! All of the toys had been put back in their places and there wasn't a broken thing in sight. The nursery assistant was singing to herself as she put a perfect copy of *Cinderella* back on the bookshelf.

Outside it was just the same. The garden looked perfect! The children were playing happily on the lawn, sharing their toys beautifully.

"Good-bye, girls." Bailey smiled, tucking the magic toy box under her

arm. "Thank you for all your help!"

"See you soon!" exclaimed Kirsty.

"And don't worry," added Rachel, "we'll keep an eye out for the other two magic items."

The best friends shared a secret smile, then ran over to find Tom and Lily.

"Now," laughed Kirsty, scooping the twins up in a big hug, "let's go back to the lodge and build some sand castles!"

Picnics
in Peril

Contents

A Brand-New Day

"Morning, Kirsty!" said Rachel, throwing back her covers.

"Morning!" exclaimed Kirsty. "Did you sleep well?"

Rachel nodded happily. Although her bed was comfy and soft, she had already been awake for ages. She couldn't wait to find out what the day had in store!

It was the girls' first morning waking

up at EcoWorld. Sunshine streamed in through the window. Kirsty stretched on her tiptoes. She could already hear the clinking of cereal bowls and the *ker-chunk* of bread popping out of the toaster in the kitchen next door.

"Do you think we'll see Bailey today?" asked Rachel, pulling on denim shorts and a purple T-shirt.

"I hope so!" replied Kirsty.

"Jack Frost's goblins still have two of her magic objects."

Rachel frowned. Until the magic

lunch bag and night-light were back
where they belonged in the Fairyland
Nursery, poor Bailey would have a
hard time looking after the fairy babies
in her care.

As the friends combed their hair and
brushed their teeth, they couldn't help
wondering where the objects might be. It
was tempting to run up and down the
EcoWorld park prodding every bush and
peering into every corner, but they knew
that wouldn't work. Queen Titania had
once told Kirsty and Rachel that they
should always let fairy magic come to
them. She'd also given each girl a
precious gold locket filled with magical
fairy dust. The smallest sprinkle turned
them into fairies whenever their help was
needed.

"Let's get some cornflakes," suggested Rachel. "Lily and Tom should be up by now."

The girls bounded into the kitchen to find both twins fastened into their high chairs.

"Kirsty!" squealed Tom, kicking his legs in delight.

Lily's rosy cheeks creased into happy  dimples as she cooed, "Ra-ra!"

"She's trying to say my name!" said Rachel, clapping her hands. "Good job, Lily!"

Mrs. Robinson wiped some mashed banana out of the pocket in Lily's bib and handed the twins some toast triangles.

"I wish the twins were as good at eating their breakfast." She sighed. "They usually love bananas, but they're more interested in throwing them across the room today."

Kirsty and Rachel poured themselves a bowl of cereal each. They sat down at the breakfast table, opposite the twins. Maybe if Tom and Lily saw *them* eating nicely the toddlers might be tempted to do the same!

"What would you like to do today, girls?" asked Mr. Walker, using his cup of coffee to hold down the edge of a foldout map. He picked up his coffee cup and pushed the map across the table for the girls to look at.

"There's kayaking, mountain biking, and archery." Mr. Tate grinned. "I want to try sailing!"

"Me too," Mrs. Tate chimed in brightly. "The beginners' lesson starts at noon."

"The lake looks stunning," added Mr. Robinson. "Kelly and I are up for sailing, aren't we?"

Mrs. Robinson seemed interested, until she remembered that she'd booked the family on a rain forest walk at the same time.

"It's being run by the Sunnydays Kids' Club," she explained. "There's going to be a trail to follow and a picnic in the center of the dome. Tom and Lily would love it. . . ."

Rachel and Kirsty exchanged excited glances. They'd both had exactly the same idea!

"Why don't we take the twins on the walk?" suggested Kirsty. "You can join us after your sailing lesson."

"They'd have a great time with us,"
piped up Rachel, giving Lily a little
wink.

Mr. and Mrs. Robinson smiled
gratefully at the girls—the offer was too
good to refuse!

They spent the next hour buzzing
around the eco-lodge,
tying shoes and
filling up
backpacks.
Kirsty
rummaged
through a
wooden chest
and pulled out an
extra picnic blanket.

"Let's go shake it in the yard," she
suggested to Rachel.

The girls skipped outside, laughing as
the blanket swished and flapped in the
fresh air. As it unfurled, the leaves on
the weeping willow at the bottom of the
yard seemed to sing along with the
gentle morning breeze.

"Look!" gasped Rachel, blinking in surprise.

A tiny fairy had tumbled out of the bottom of the picnic blanket! Bailey shook her golden hair, waved her wand, then darted into the air.

"Hello!" she called. "I came as soon as I heard about the children's picnic. It's more important than ever that we find the magic lunch bag!"

"You can count on us," replied Kirsty. "We'll be on the lookout."

Bailey's eyes brightened. "Thank you,

girls! I'll flutter back to Fairyland and keep watch there. We're having a picnic for the fairy babies today, too. . . ."

Before Bailey could say another word, footsteps padded along the walkway at the bottom of the yard. Rachel clutched Kirsty's arm. The first children were making their way to the rain forest zone!

"If we want to stop the goblins from causing trouble," she warned, "we should go right now!"

Trails and Tracks

"There you are, girls! The twins are all ready."

Bailey had only just disappeared when Mrs. Robinson pushed the double stroller out onto the patio. Tom and Lily both waved, their little faces rosy with excitement.

"Whew!" whispered Kirsty, giving Rachel a secret nudge. "That was close!"

The tiniest trace of scarlet fairy dust still shimmered in the air around them, but Mrs. Robinson didn't seem to notice. She was busy loading the stroller up with spare clothes, wipes, and toys.

"I won't be long," she promised, flashing Kirsty and Rachel a grateful smile.

"There's no rush," replied Kirsty. "Enjoy the sailing!"

Rachel crouched down to grin at each of the twins, before adding, "We're going to have our own adventure, aren't we?"

"Yes, Ra-ra!" piped up Tom and Lily.

As soon as Mrs. Robinson had kissed
the toddlers good-bye, the friends
unlatched the gate and wheeled the
double stroller out onto the forest trail.
The wooden walkway twisted in and out
of the trees, curving past eco-lodges and
leafy camping spots. Soon, the rain forest
dome appeared, creepers and vines
curling up inside its glass windows.

The dome entrance was bustling with people. Babies peeked out of carriers, toddlers played tag around their moms' legs, and grandparents took pictures with their cameras. A worker stood at the doorway dressed in a Sunnydays Kids' Club T-shirt with a big smiley face printed on the front.

"There's Diane," said Kirsty.

"She seems much happier now that the goblin has left," added Rachel.

"Hello, Lily. Hello, Tom," said Diane, checking their names off her list. "We're almost ready to start our walk!"

Kirsty and Rachel parked the stroller and unfastened the twins. Diane held up her special Sunnydays flag, and everybody gathered around.

"Welcome to our wonderful rain forest," she announced. "You're free to explore the whole dome. The routes are full of animals, insects, and flowers."

"Make sure you stay

close," said Kirsty, reaching for the twins' hands.

"Good advice," praised Diane. "The dome is enormous—in fact it's a whole mini ecosystem! Luckily, every path leads to the waterfall in the center. That's where we're going to have our Sunnydays picnic."

"Utterby! Utterby!" cooed Lily, tugging at Kirsty's hand. A butterfly with shimmering turquoise wings fluttered over the children's heads.

"OK," Kirsty chuckled. "We'll follow the 'utterby'!"

Diane handed Rachel a sketchbook and some colored pencils. There were

five fun things for the twins to look for in
the dome—a frog, a seed, a feather, a
petal, and a butterfly.

"I wonder if Tom and Lily can draw a
picture of all five," Diane said with a
smile.

At that moment, the turquoise butterfly
settled on the end of her clipboard. The
twins squealed with delight.
They'd found
one thing on
the list
already! Soon
the pair was
scampering
up and down
the rain forest paths,

peeking through ferns and picking up
pebbles.

"Look! Frog!" cried Tom a few minutes later.

A tiny frog sat on the tip of a palm leaf, no bigger than a fairy. It looked up at the little boy and blinked.

"Isn't it sweet?" exclaimed Rachel, drawing a frog shape for Lily to color in.

"I found something here, too," cried Kirsty.

"Is it a seed?" asked Rachel. "Or maybe a feather?"

Kirsty shook her head. There in the soil

was the outline of an enormous, webbed foot. Only one creature that she could think of would leave a mark like that.

"Oh, Rachel," she gasped. "It's got to be a goblin footprint!"

Picnic Problems

"Where are my bogmallows?" yelled an unfriendly voice.

"Don't ask me," snapped another. "What did that fairy say? 'Picnics are wonderful'? Ha!"

Rachel gulped. There really were goblins nearby!

The shouting got louder and louder.

"No bogmallows anywhere? Terrible! *Terrible!*"

Kirsty leaped to her feet, her face pale with worry. The goblins were making so much noise they must be lurking right around the next bend.

"Me look?" trilled Tom, toddling after Kirsty.

Rachel scooped Tom up and stepped back toward the path. "We can't do anything while we're babysitting," she reminded her friend. "Let's take the twins to the picnic area. Mr. and Mrs. Robinson's lesson should be finished by now."

"It's that way," agreed Kirsty. "We'll get there faster if we give the twins a piggyback ride."

Lily and Tom
giggled and
cheered as the
girls carried
them over
stepping stones,
stooped under
vines, and waded through swishy rushes.

"I can hear splashing," exclaimed
Rachel. "We must be getting close."

The trail curved one last time, then
opened out onto a clearing in the very
heart of the dome. A stunning waterfall
tumbled over a tower of rocks, little
rainbows dancing in the spray. All
around the edge, tropical orchids
blossomed in hot shades of tangerine,
scarlet, and pink. It was the perfect
location for a rain forest picnic.

"Mommy! Daddy!" cried Lily, scrambling down from Kirsty's back.

"Oh, my," said Kirsty in a low voice. "What happened here?"

The picnic area was in chaos. The Sunnydays team had set out a delicious spread, but half of the tables had collapsed, sending trays of sandwiches and cupcakes spilling to the ground. Mrs.

Tate and Mrs. Walker were laying down picnic blankets, but they were splattered with mud. Diane rushed around in a panic trying to find something for the hungry children to eat.

"It's a disaster!" she cried, rescuing a squashed plate of pigs in blankets.

Kirsty squeezed Rachel's arm.

"Look at those pigs in blankets," she whispered. "The pastry's turned green!"

Rachel gasped. Kirsty was right! Every pig in a blanket had a horrible green tinge to it, and so did the cupcakes.

"We have to track down those goblins," Rachel urged. "They're ruining the food!"

Kirsty and Rachel handed the twins back to Mrs. Robinson, then ran off to find their parents.

"We had a great time on the lake." Mr. Tate sighed. "But things have taken a turn for the worse!"

Mr. Walker looked down at his shoe and groaned. "Now I've stepped in pudding. How did that happen?"

"Do you mind if we take a walk?" asked Rachel.

Mr. Walker wiped the pudding off his shoe. "You go on, girls. We've got *plenty* to do here."

Within minutes, Kirsty and Rachel were running back down the trail.

"Let's hide here," whispered Rachel, slipping behind a tree.

Kirsty peeked through the branches, then ducked back out of sight. Three grumpy goblins were sitting on tree stumps just a few feet away from them! They were making a terrible racket.

"Give me that!" demanded one, swiping a teapot from his friend and drinking from the spout.

"How rude!" snapped another, erupting into a giant goblin burp. "I bet those yucky fairy babies have enough drinks and snacks at their picnics!"

The third goblin sat with a messy tablecloth tied around his neck, rubbing his bloated belly.

"It's too hot in here," he groaned. "I feel icky. . . ."

"You only feel sick because you ate all the food," grumbled the burping goblin.

The first goblin put down his teapot and began to chuckle.

"At least we spoiled Bailey's fun." He laughed. "She'll never guess where we've stashed her lunch bag."

Kirsty and Rachel took a step closer and listened carefully.

"Hiding it in Fairyland was a brilliant idea," he continued. "It's right under their noses."

The ill goblin wiped his mouth with the back of his hand.

"I'm tired of this," he announced. "Let's go back and get it. When we hand over the lunch bag, Jack Frost is bound to give us a reward!"

Kirsty and Rachel froze on the spot, their eyes wide with worry. There was only one thing to do—they had to get to Fairyland first!

Off to Fairyland!

The goblins stomped out of the clearing, pushing and shoving one another through the bushes. As soon as the coast was clear, Kirsty and Rachel leaped out from their hiding spot.

"Poor Bailey," Kirsty said. "We have to warn her."

Rachel reached for her gold necklace and carefully opened the locket. Inside was a sprinkling of fairy dust.

"Let's hold hands," she suggested, as Kirsty opened her locket, too.

The best friends scattered a pinch of fairy dust into the air. A sweet-scented breeze instantly began to curl around their legs.

"Isn't it beautiful?" marveled Kirsty, as the breeze transformed into a trail of exquisite rainbow colors. The enchanted rainbow swirled around the girls, and lifted them high into the air.

Kirsty and Rachel felt a tickle on their shoulders. A pair of shimmering fairy wings had appeared

on each girl's back! The girls fluttered
their wings and laughed. It was
wonderful to be fairies again!

After a while, the rainbow began to
arch back toward the ground. Kirsty and
Rachel found themselves floating toward
a wood dotted with blossoming trees.
When their feet touched the grass, the
rainbow faded away as quickly as it had
arrived.

"Where are we?"
wondered Rachel,
breathing in
the country
air. "I don't
think we've
visited this
part of
Fairyland before."

Kirsty pointed to a toadstool cottage with sunflowers growing in the garden. She fluttered up the path to the front door.

"Come here, Rachel!" she gasped, as soon as she got to the front door.

Above the bell, a hand-painted sign read FAIRY BABYSITTER. The girls had discovered the Fairyland Nursery!

Kirsty stepped forward and rang the bell. A happy chime pealed across the wood, but no one answered. She was just about to turn away when Rachel pointed to a little path leading around the cottage. "I can hear voices," she whispered.

Kirsty and Rachel followed the path to the back of the cottage.

"How adorable!" Rachel gasped. "Look!"

There, at the bottom of the garden, was a circle of fairy babies. They sat like cherubs, their delicate gossamer wings twinkling in the sunlight. The babies were dressed in footed pajamas and little floppy sunhats. Each one clutched a wand with a glowing star at the very tip.

"Those must be training wands," guessed Kirsty.

"I can see Bailey, too," added Rachel.

Bailey was struggling to open a picnic basket packed full of food. The girls fluttered up in the nick of time. Just as they joined the circle, the basket fell facedown onto the lawn!

"Oh, dear." Bailey sighed, watching as cupcakes, rolls, and apples tumbled across the grass. "I should have known this might happen!" "We can help," offered Kirsty. Bailey tried to greet her friends with a smile, but her sweet face was full of worry. "Our picnic hasn't gotten off to a very good start," she confessed. "Without the magic lunch bag, none of the food tastes very good."

Just then another fairy fluttered down the path. Kirsty and Rachel recognized

the strawberry curls
and shimmering blue
vest right away—
it was Polly the
Party Fun Fairy!
"I'm here to
organize the picnic
party games," Polly
explained, "but they
keep going wrong! The donkey for Pin
the Tail on the Donkey wandered away.
Even the balloons have gone flat."

"We overheard the goblins talking,"
announced Rachel. "The magic lunch
bag is in Fairyland . . . and they're
coming to get it!"

"We have to find it first," replied
Bailey. "If Jack Frost steals the lunch bag
back, all snacks will be ruined!"

"I'll babysit while you search," Polly offered kindly.

"Where should we start?" asked Rachel, darting up toward the cottage as fast as her wings could carry her.

Kirsty thought hard. The goblin had said that he'd hidden the lunch bag right under the fairies' noses. What did he mean?

Suddenly, her face lit up.

"Bailey," she said, "can you show us inside the Fairyland Nursery? I think the goblins played a trick on us."

Lost, then Found

"This way!" cried Bailey.

Kirsty and Rachel followed her through a quaint red kitchen, up a twisting set of stairs, and into the nursery playroom.

"It's just as magical as I knew it would be," exclaimed Rachel, remembering the pictures Bailey had revealed in the Seeing Pool only a day before.

Kirsty flitted past the row of tiny cribs and sweet fairy teddy bears.

"That goblin hid the lunch bag where a fairy would never think of looking," she remarked. "Where do you keep your magic objects, Bailey?"

Bailey pointed to a bookshelf tucked away in the farthest corner of the playroom. Three quilted cushions were neatly lined up along the top shelf. The first one had the magic toy box on top.

"Look underneath the middle one," urged Rachel.

Bailey darted up to the top shelf and lifted up the cushion. Suddenly, her wand began to fizz with scarlet stars!

"It's here!" she cried, pulling out the magic lunch bag.

Rachel and Kirsty beamed at each other. Trust the silly goblins to hide it in plain sight!

"Well done." Bailey laughed, bursting into a peal of fairy giggles. "Let's tell Polly."

The delighted fairy opened the playroom window and called down to the garden.

"Now picnics everywhere can be fun

again," added Rachel, thinking of Lily
and Tom in the rain forest dome.

"Not if I can help it!" bellowed a voice.

Kirsty and Rachel shivered in surprise
as bony green fingers plucked the lunch
bag out of Bailey's hands.

"It's the goblin from the picnic!" cried
Kirsty.

The greedy goblin
smirked. The
mischievous
creature had
climbed in
through the
toadstool's
window.

"That's me!" he
boasted. "This lunch bag is going to live
in Jack Frost's Ice Castle."

"No," cried Bailey. "Please give it back!"

The goblin guffawed loudly.

"We've got to do something," said Kirsty breathlessly.

Rachel fluttered up to the ceiling. She circled around and around the playroom, leaving a trail of fairy dust shimmering in the air behind her. The goblin stumbled and shouted, swiping at her with his free hand.

"Stop it!" he groaned. "You're making me dizzy!"

"Faster," urged Kirsty, her eyes twinkling with delight.

Rachel looped again and again. The
angry goblin lunged at her
but missed, tripping into
a fairy crib instead.
When he got back
to his feet, there
was a dainty lace
curtain caught on
one of his pointy ears.

Kirsty spotted her chance.

"Give us back the lunch bag now," she
demanded.

"No!" pouted the goblin. "I want a
reward from Jack Frost."

Bailey bravely stepped a little closer.
"I've got an even better reward," she
said. "How would you like a stinky
goblin picnic full of gross foods?"

"You wouldn't have to share," added Kirsty.

"That's right!" piped up Rachel. "Smelly cauliflower, rotten eggs, and a pile of bogmallows. It's all yours."

The greedy goblin paused for a moment to lick his lips.

"Nah," he decided. "I don't trust you fairies!"

With that, the goblin tucked the magic lunch bag under his arm and flung open the playroom door.

The thief howled in panic. A group of fairy babies was fluttering up the stairs!

The little tots gurgled at the sight of the funny-looking stranger. Some even held their arms out for a hug.

"Don't you like fairy babies?" Rachel asked innocently.

The goblin shuffled nervously from foot to foot.

"They're just as cute as human ones," said Kirsty. She knew that goblins were afraid of human babies.

"Horrible things, all of them," he yowled, pressing the magic lunch bag into Bailey's hands. "Keep your precious object. I'm leaving!"

The goblin marched out of the playroom, slamming the door behind him.

Bang!

The fairies were delighted. Bailey held

her arms out, wrapping each of the little kids in a hug.

"Let's start the picnic all over again," she said. "Kirsty, Rachel, will you join us?"

The best friends shared a smile.

"Not this time," replied Kirsty. "Two very special babies are waiting for us in the human world."

"That's right," Rachel agreed. "We can't be late for the rain forest picnic!"

The Stolen Night-light

Contents

Lanterns by the Lake

"What good sticking, Tom," said Kirsty with a smile. "Good job!"

Rachel crouched down to admire Lily's handiwork.

"Look!" she exclaimed. "Lily's almost ready to start painting."

It was Kirsty and Rachel's last full day at EcoWorld, and the friends were eager to make the most of every minute.

After breakfast they'd brought the twins down to the lake. Diane from the Sunnydays Kids' Club was running an outdoor craft session.

"This really is a perfect spot, isn't it?" Rachel sighed happily.

"Bliss!" agreed Kirsty. "And making recycled paper lanterns is such a great idea."

The man-made lake was set in the middle of an airy dome fitted with a special roof that could be pulled back on dry days like today. Diane had set up a row of tables along the lake's sandy beach. A dozen happy children sat clutching glue sticks, crayons, glitter, and tape.

"Ra-ra!" squealed Lily, finding a

paintbrush and pointing to the pink
paint. "You do it?"

"Let's decorate it together," suggested
Rachel. "What would you like to paint
on your lantern?"

Sweet little dimples suddenly appeared
in Lily's cheeks.

"Fairies!" she squealed. "Lily like
fairies!"

"I like fairies, too." Rachel smiled,
catching Kirsty's eye.

With her golden curls and polka-dot pinafore dress, Lily reminded the friends of the adorable fairy babies in Bailey the Babysitter Fairy's nursery. All she needed was a star-topped training wand and a tiny pair of fairy wings!

While Rachel and Lily were painting, Kirsty helped Tom tape up the sides of his lantern. "We'll come back to the lake later and watch them fly high into the air," she explained.

"Higher than me?" wondered Tom, his eyes open wide.

Kirsty laughed. "Yes, much higher than you!"

Diane wandered up to see how the children were doing.

"The roof is going to stay open this evening," she said. "The lanterns will float right up to the sky! There's going to be a barbecue and  songs around the campfire."

Tom and Lily beamed at each other. It sounded magical!

"I just hope that Jack Frost doesn't spoil their fun," Rachel murmured under her breath. "Bailey is still missing one magic object."

Kirsty frowned. Without Bailey's night-light, children's nap times were sure to go terribly wrong.

"Let's take the twins for a walk around the park," she suggested. "We might spot a clue."

"Good idea!" replied Rachel.

The girls wrote the twins' names on their lanterns, then laid them out to dry. After letting Diane know where they were going, they wandered down the boardwalk that led out to the main park.

"Where do we start?" wondered Rachel.

She squinted up at a wooden post with signs pointing in every direction. Should they try the rain forest dome, the Treetop Café, or the eco-center?

Just then, a hoot of laughter echoed through the trees.

"Hurry up!" yelled a voice.

"Stop pushing!" shouted another. "I'm getting in there first!"

Rachel reached for Tom's and Lily's hands.

The yelling got louder and louder. Kirsty had heard that sort of noise before . . . from goblins!

The best friends felt their hearts thump as the bushes began to rustle and shake. Three shadowy figures burst through the trees. The rowdy group was all dressed in wetsuits reaching way down to their ankles. Kirsty and Rachel peered at the strangers' feet, searching for a glimpse of green.

"This way!" yelled a boy with blond hair, pointing to a sign that read SPLASH PARK.

"Awesome!" cheered his friend, shoving to the front.

Rachel sighed. These weren't goblins at all! It was just a bunch of boys on their way to the swimming center.

"Where now?" asked Kirsty, putting her hands on her hips. "Tom and Lily's nap time is soon. We can't let Jack Frost ruin their last day at EcoWorld!"

Nap Nuisance

"The twins are starting to look sleepy," said Rachel, leading Tom and Lily back onto the path.

"Want Mommy," said Tom, holding out his arms to be carried. Lily trailed behind her brother, sucking her thumb.

"Let's take them back to the lodge," suggested Kirsty. "We might find something on the way."

"Would you like another piggyback ride?" asked Rachel.

Tom nodded sleepily.

The girls lifted the twins onto their backs, then slowly made their way along the trail.

"Hello, girls!" Mr. Tate grinned as the friends finally trooped through the gate at the bottom of the yard. "You're just in time for lunch."

Mr. and Mrs. Walker looked up from their lounge chairs and waved. Mrs. Tate placed a big bowl of pasta in the middle of the picnic table.

"Thank you for taking Tom and Lily out." Mrs. Robinson smiled, putting down her magazine.

"I'd better get the twins into their cribs right away," she said. "We want them to have lots of energy for the campfire and barbecue tonight!"

"Can we help?" asked Rachel, running in to find Lily's favorite rag doll.

Mrs. Robinson nodded. "That would be great, thank you."

Kirsty and Rachel carried Tom and Lily into their bedroom. Mrs. Robinson

drew the curtains, while the girls clipped
the twins into their fleecy sleeping bags.
It was a perfect room for a nap—baby
rabbits scampered and hopped along the
wallpaper and rainbow mobiles spun
gently from the ceiling.

"Night-night," whispered Rachel.

"No, Ra-ra!" squealed Lily, sitting up again.

Rachel tried to lay the little girl back down, but she clenched her fists and refused. At the same time, Tom reached for the crib bars and pulled himself up.

"No sleeps!" he called, bouncing up and down on the mattress. "This isn't like them," said Mrs. Robinson, searching for the twins' night-light. "They usually love their lunchtime nap."

Rachel tried to comfort Lily, but the

toddler shook her head and threw her
doll onto the carpet. Tom clung on to the
crib bars and began to cry.

Mrs. Robinson rummaged through the
twins' closets.

"Where has that night-light gone?" she
asked out loud. "Lily and Tom love the
lullabies it plays."

The twins began to sob even more
loudly. Mrs. Robinson looked relieved
when Mr. Robinson stuck his head
around the door to find out what all the
fuss was about.

"We'll leave you to
settle the twins,"
suggested Rachel,
sharing a knowing
look with Kirsty.

The friends
rushed out to
the yard so
they could talk
properly.

"The twins won't settle down until
Bailey's magic night-light is back where
it belongs," said Kirsty. "We have to
keep looking!"

The girls checked with their parents, then hurried out to the park. As they ran along the trail, they could hear babies crying in the other eco-lodges.

"She can't nap without her night-light!" they heard one frazzled mom call.

"He won't even shut his eyes," insisted another dad, pacing up and down his yard with a baby in a sling.

"This is serious," said Rachel urgently. "None of the children can get to sleep!"

"Let's head back to the forest," suggested Kirsty.

She climbed over a root, then darted into a pretty tunnel of willow trees. The branches seemed to bend and curve toward them, hiding the girls from view.

"Look behind you," whispered Rachel.

Kirsty spun around. Somehow, the branches had closed over the entrance to the path! The girls found themselves standing in a secret den covered in fluttering green leaves.

"My fingers are tingling!" Kirsty gasped.

"Oh, Kirsty," marveled Rachel. "We're being called to Fairyland!"

Trouble at Twilight

A burst of glittering light swirled around Kirsty and Rachel, spinning the girls around and around. The willow branches began to sway, their leaves shimmering in green and gold.

Kirsty felt her toes lift off the path. "We're shrinking to fairy-size!" she cried.

Rachel smiled, then reached for her best friend's hand.

At that moment, a delicate pair of

gossamer wings appeared on each girl's shoulders. The willow trees parted again, and the girls fluttered out into the warm afternoon sunlight.

A moment later, the girls were standing in a country garden dotted with beautiful golden sunflowers. A long

curved path led up to an enchanting toadstool cottage. "It's the Fairyland Nursery!" exclaimed Kirsty. A fairy with curly black hair opened a window and peered outside.

"I'm so thrilled to see you again!" she called. "Come in."

When Rachel and Kirsty got to the back door, they recognized Sabrina the Sweet Dreams Fairy. The friends shared a warm hug—they had fond memories of the time they helped Sabrina and the Night Fairies get their bags of magic dust back from Jack Frost.

"Follow me, girls," Sabrina said

hastily. "Bailey needs your help."

Rachel and Kirsty fluttered down the hallway as quickly as they could. When they got to the playroom, they couldn't believe their eyes. There were fairy babies climbing up the canopies, hiding in toy boxes, and crawling under shelves. The other Night Fairies were rushing up and down trying to coax the little ones back into their cribs. Even Nia the Night Owl Fairy's magic bag of sleep dust

didn't seem to be working. Poor Bailey
stood in the middle of the chaos,
clutching a pile of pillows.

Poof!

Suddenly, the pillows that Bailey had
been carrying changed into a stack of
silly dress-up clothes. A little fairy in
striped pajamas had crawled up and
touched it with her star-topped wand!

"Please *try* and remember the rules,

Ellie," sighed Bailey, putting the funny hats and frilly dresses onto a chair. "No magic at naptime."

The baby peered up at Bailey and then burst into a peal of fairy giggles. It was impossible to be upset with her, but poor Bailey's face looked tired and sad.

"If fairy babies miss their sleep, their spells start going haywire," she explained. "When Morgan came by to help this afternoon, a stray bolt of baby magic turned her hair blue! It will take hours to fade back to normal again."

Morgan the Midnight Fairy peeked her head out from underneath a nearby crib. The fairy's lovely blonde hair had turned as blue as her dress!

Rachel squeezed Bailey's hand. "What can we do to help?" she asked.

"We have to get my night-light back before bedtime," replied the flustered fairy. "Missing a nap is one thing, but who knows what will happen if none of the babies sleep tonight!"

Kirsty thought for a moment. "If the night-light isn't in Fairyland or the human world, then there's only one place left to try," she announced. "Jack Frost's Ice Castle!"

Into the Ice Castle

"Hold on tight, everyone!" called Bailey.
"Please try and stay in line."

Kirsty and Rachel smiled at each
other. It was hard to believe that they
were fluttering through the sky hand in
hand with a dozen adorable fairy babies!
When the friends had decided to go to
the Ice Castle, Bailey thought it best to
bring the little ones along, too, so she

could look after them. The Night Fairies couldn't babysit any longer, as they had to get ready for their night's work.

"Don't let go of my hand," Kirsty whispered gently into the ear of a tiny fairy with dancing green eyes.

The toddler flipped onto her tummy, then burst into tinkling giggles. Fairy

babies could fly, and they couldn't resist
zooming off in zigzags or dizzy loop-the-
loops. Bailey had to remind all the
babies to fly in a row so that no one got
lost. Kirsty was posted at one end of the
flying line and Rachel at the other.
Bailey flew in the middle of the line, so
she could keep an eye on everyone.

Suddenly, way off in the distance, they could see the spiky silhouette of Jack Frost's Ice Castle. As the fairies got closer, the air turned cold. Soon they were fluttering around the castle's icy turrets.

"Let's slip in here," suggested Rachel, pointing to a narrow window.

Bailey waved her wand and whispered a spell, making the fairies so small that they could slip into the castle unseen.

She hushed the fairy babies, who thought being

silent was a wonderful new game.

The group fluttered through the castle's gloomy corridors without making a sound. Rachel took the lead, darting left and right as they fluttered past dungeons, kitchens, and icy staircases. There wasn't a goblin in sight.

"Here's the Throne Room," breathed Kirsty, approaching an enormous pair of wrought-iron doors.

Bailey called all the fairy babies around her and asked them to listen carefully.

"Everyone fly up near the ceiling, please," she said. "It's important to stay out of sight."

The fairies darted into the Throne
Room through a tiny gap in the door.
Hordes of goblins
were lying on
the stone floor,
dressed in
nightshirts
or pajamas.
Each had a
little night-
light beside
them, but
not a single
one was sleeping.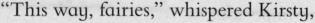
Instead, they were throwing blankets
around, sticking out their tongues, or
spurting hot chocolate everywhere!

"This way, fairies," whispered Kirsty,

pointing up to the ceiling. "Hide up there!"

The fairy babies fluttered up to the crystal chandelier in the center of the Throne Room, their little eyes full of wonder.

"What was that?" barked a goblin, feeling a tiny breeze rush past his nose.

"Don't ask me!" bellowed his friend, whacking another goblin in the head with a pillow. "Take this instead!"

The goblin next to him tried to get up and fight back, but his big green feet were caught in his sleeping bag. The goblin landed on his friends with a noisy thump, sending night-lights scattering in all directions.

Up on the chandelier, the fairy babies collapsed into delighted giggles. They thought it was the funniest thing they'd ever seen!

"Those night-lights must have been stolen from the human world," Rachel told Kirsty.

"My magic night-light's here, too," whispered Bailey. "Look!"

She pointed at Jack Frost's ice-blue throne in the center of the room. Jack Frost himself was slumped in the seat, holding the magic night-light! But he looked thoroughly miserable.

"Why won't this thing work?" he grumbled, giving the night-light a hard shake. "Silly fairy magic!"

149

The friends flew as close to Jack Frost as they dared. As soon as Bailey set her tiny feet on the top of his throne, the magic night-light began to glow. A sweet lullaby started to play. Jack Frost leaped to his feet in surprise.

"What are you doing here?" he thundered as he spotted the fairies.

"I'm here for the night-light," Bailey said boldly. "It belongs to me."

Jack Frost snatched up the magic night-

light, then dangled it over the side of the throne with one bony finger. The fairy babies on the chandelier shrieked in surprise.

"It's useless!" he snapped. "I thought your silly objects would help make my goblins behave, but none of them worked. I'm going to smash the night-light!"

Bedtime at Last

"The night-light only works for true babysitters," explained Bailey. "You must want the children in your care to be safe and happy, *not* just to obey your every command!"

"Ha!" barked Jack Frost, turning his back and sulking.

Kirsty and Rachel spotted their chance. The friends darted forward and Rachel grabbed the night-light.

"Bailey!" called Rachel, tossing the enchanted object through the air. "Catch!"

As soon as it landed in Bailey's arms, the magic night-light began to glow even brighter, casting shapes across the Throne Room walls.

Jack Frost's face turned white with rage. He swiped at Bailey but missed, landing in a furious heap.

"Goblins!" he screeched. "Get those pesky fairies!"

Kirsty nudged Rachel in the ribs. "Jack Frost's goblins aren't listening!"

Now that the magic night-light was working again, the fairy babies had fluttered down from the chandelier. The little ones were trying to snuggle in the blankets next to the goblins! Instead of grabbing the fairies, Jack Frost's goblins were wailing pitifully and scrambling to get away.

"*Ugh!*" yelled one. "This one's trying to hug me. Get it off!"

"Help!" yelled another, trying to shake an adorable fairy toddler off his sleeping bag.

"Of course!" Rachel grinned. "Goblins can't stand babies—human or fairy ones!"

"Luckily, babies *love* goblins!" replied Kirsty.

A terrified goblin glanced up at the pretty shadows the night-light was casting on the castle walls.

"It gets worse!" he shouted, pointing at the silhouettes. "Now giant Pogwurzels are coming to get us!"

The room dissolved into shrieking as panicked goblins fled in every direction. Jack Frost sat in the  middle with his face in his hands.

"It's nearly fairy bedtime," said Bailey. "Should we go home?"

Once the fairy babies were all settled in their cribs back at the Fairyland

Nursery, Bailey sat down to read them a bedtime story.

"Why don't we have *Spikilocks and the Three Goblins,*" suggested Bailey, touching an old leather covered book with her wand.

Kirsty and Rachel watched spellbound as a parade of tiny storybook characters tripped through the air above the babies' heads. The story was so enchanting, even they couldn't help feeling a little sad when Bailey closed the book and said it was the end.

"Sweet dreams," smiled Kirsty, fluttering from crib to crib.

"It was magical meeting you," added Rachel, kissing each of the babies good night.

Bailey turned on her night-light, filling the room with a warm glow. A lovely lullaby began to play.

"I can't thank you enough," she whispered, wrapping the girls in a tight hug. "Now little ones everywhere can be happy and safe again!"

"And we've got some babysitting to do tonight," said Kirsty. "Don't we, Rachel?"

Rachel thought of Lily and Tom. The friends couldn't miss their last night in the lodge!

"I'll send you to nighttime in the human world," said Bailey. "Good-bye, girls!"

Kirsty and Rachel held hands and shut their eyes tight. When they opened them again, they were back to normal size and standing by the side of the lake in EcoWorld. A stunning silver moon shone down on the water, a thousand tiny stars twinkling brightly behind it.

"Lantern time!" cried Tom, wrapping his arms around Kirsty's legs, as the girls wandered up to the Tates, Walkers, and Robinsons.

Lily squealed with pleasure. "Ra-ra!" she grinned, holding out her paper lantern.

Rachel gasped. The lanterns had been transformed. Each one sparkled in the moonlight, glinting with tiny gemstones and pearls.

"It must be fairy magic," whispered Kirsty to Rachel, as she lifted Tom into her arms.

Mrs. Robinson came over to the girls. "Enjoy the magical sight!" She smiled. "Afterward we'll put the little ones to bed."

Rachel beamed at Kirsty. She had a feeling that the twins were going to sleep well tonight!

Don't miss any of Rachel and Kirsty's
other fairy adventures!
Join them as they try to help

Nicole
the Beach Fairy!

Read on for a special sneak peek. . . .

Time for Action

"Isn't it wonderful to be back on Rainspell Island again, Rachel?" Kirsty Tate said happily, gazing out over the shimmering blue-green sea. "It hasn't changed a bit!"

Rachel Walker, Kirsty's best friend, nodded. "Rainspell is still as beautiful as ever," she replied as the two girls followed the rocky path down to the beach. "This is one of the most special places in the whole world!"

The Tates and the Walkers were spending school break on Rainspell Island. Even though it was fall, the sky was a clear blue and the sun was shining brightly, so it felt more like summer. Kirsty and Rachel couldn't wait to get to the beach and dip their toes in the ocean.

"You're right, Rachel," Kirsty agreed, her eyes twinkling. "After all, this is where we first became friends!"

"And we found lots of other amazing friends here, too, didn't we?" Rachel laughed.

Kirsty and Rachel shared a magical secret. During their first visit to Rainspell Island, they'd met the Rainbow Fairies, who had been cast out of Fairyland by Jack Frost's wicked spell. Since then, the girls had gotten to know many of the other fairies.

RAINBOW magic™

Which Magical Fairies Have You Met?

- ❑ The Rainbow Fairies
- ❑ The Weather Fairies
- ❑ The Jewel Fairies
- ❑ The Pet Fairies
- ❑ The Dance Fairies
- ❑ The Music Fairies
- ❑ The Sports Fairies
- ❑ The Party Fairies
- ❑ The Ocean Fairies
- ❑ The Night Fairies
- ❑ The Magical Animal Fairies
- ❑ The Princess Fairies
- ❑ The Superstar Fairies
- ❑ The Fashion Fairies
- ❑ The Sugar & Spice Fairies
- ❑ The Earth Fairies

◼SCHOLASTIC

Find all of your favorite fairy friends at
scholastic.com/rainbowmagic

HIT entertainment

RMFAIRY10

RAINBOW magic™

SPECIAL EDITION

Which Magical Fairies Have You Met?

3 stories in each one!

- ❑ Joy the Summer Vacation Fairy
- ❑ Holly the Christmas Fairy
- ❑ Kylie the Carnival Fairy
- ❑ Stella the Star Fairy
- ❑ Shannon the Ocean Fairy
- ❑ Trixie the Halloween Fairy
- ❑ Gabriella the Snow Kingdom Fairy
- ❑ Juliet the Valentine Fairy
- ❑ Mia the Bridesmaid Fairy
- ❑ Flora the Dress-Up Fairy
- ❑ Paige the Christmas Play Fairy
- ❑ Emma the Easter Fairy
- ❑ Cara the Camp Fairy
- ❑ Destiny the Rock Star Fairy
- ❑ Belle the Birthday Fairy
- ❑ Olympia the Games Fairy
- ❑ Selena the Sleepover Fairy
- ❑ Cheryl the Christmas Tree Fairy
- ❑ Florence the Friendship Fairy
- ❑ Lindsay the Luck Fairy
- ❑ Brianna the Tooth Fairy
- ❑ Autumn the Falling Leaves Fairy
- ❑ Keira the Movie Star Fairy
- ❑ Addison the April Fool's Day Fairy
- ❑ Bailey the Babysitter Fairy

▥ SCHOLASTIC

Find all of your favorite fairy friends at
scholastic.com/rainbowmagic

HiT entertainment

RMSPECIAL13